MW00834008

THE
PRAYER DANCER

A THREE-ACT PLAY

TRACIE E. MORRISON

America Star Books
Frederick, Maryland

Softcover 9781681762845
PUBLISHED BY AMERICA STAR BOOKS, LLLP
www.americastarbooks.pub
Frederick, Maryland

INTRODUCTION

"The Prayer Dancer" is a Christian stage play for the entire family that is driven by the art of dance, rather than song. The voices of the four women you will encounter - Rachel, Amber, "Peaches"/Tamara and Joy – echo the words that I have spoken, felt, and lived over the years. Within three acts, this piece seeks to present a realistic portrayal of four women on their Christian journey, who face issues of abuse, the inability to conceive, wavering commitment to God, and insecurity about God's will, plan, and purpose for their lives. While exploring their relationship with Christ and each other, they are bound together by doubt, fear, anger, and faith. Throughout the play, dance will help tell the story, express emotions, and demonstrate a unique form of praise and worship. It is with pleasure and a humble heart that I present, "The Prayer Dancer" to you...

CHARACTERS
(in order of appearance)

RACHEL – Modern Dancer. Married to Rafiq.

RAFIQ – Corporate type, married to Rachel, abusive.

PRECIOUS – Rachel and Rafiq's 8-10 year old daughter.

AMBER – Tap Dancer. Married to Patrick.

PATRICK – Gentle and loving husband, married to Amber.

JOY – Liturgical Dancer, Michael's romantic interest.

TAMARA "PEACHES" – Hip Hop Video Dancer, struggles in her walk with God.

MICHAEL – Dancer, romantic interest in Joy.

AN AGENT

*Various other dancers may be needed to double in various places throughout.

SETTING
All of the play's action is set in the Spring of 2000.

ACT ONE

Scene 1. A WALK IN MY SHOES
Scene 2. THE PRESS
Scene 3. BLING BLING
Scene 4. THE MASK

ACT TWO
One month later.

Scene 1. I GOT ALL MY SISTERS WITH ME (THE COMPETITION)
Scene 2. LEAN ON ME/HEALING BALM
Scene 3. DANCE WITH ME
Scene 4. MY SISTER, MY FRIEND
Scene 5. HE RESTORES MY SOUL
Scene 6. LOVE DIVINE

ACT THREE
One year later.

Scene 1. A FAMILY AFFAIR
Scene 2. THE DANCER'S PRAYER

ACT ONE

SCENE ONE
A WALK IN MY SHOES

Lights reveal Joy, Amber, Rachel and Tamara positioned as statuesque sculpture or work of art center stage. A soft musical introduction plays overhead. The statue comes to life and begins to dance slow at first and then all of the women dance off leaving one lone dancer. As she moves the lights shift to reveal Rachel asleep. She tosses occasionally as she is dreaming about this dancer dancing to The Lord's Prayer. She mumbles the words of the prayer aloud simultaneous we hear it overhead.

VOICEOVER

Our father, who art in heaven, hallowed be thy name. Thy kingdom come. Thy will be done, on earth, as it is in heaven. Give us this day our daily bread and forgive us our trespasses as we forgive those who trespass against us. Lead us not into temptation but deliver us from evil. For thine is the Kingdom and the power and the glory forever. Amen. Amen. Amen.

RACHEL
(mumbles)

Our father who art…

All of sudden the door opens and slams violently and Rachel is startled. Dancer exits. Rafiq, drunk, looms in the front door. He wears the clothing from the previous day at work – a suite, which is wrinkled and the tie, crooked.

RAFIQ
(slurred yell)

RACHEL

Rafiq stumbles toward the bedroom door, knocking over the coat rack. Ignoring the rack he grabs hold of the couch to balance himself. He looks around the living room.

RAFIQ

Where are you?...I know you here me calling you...NOW ANSWER ME!

He storms through the living room to the bedroom. Rachel turns over to see Rafiq in the doorway.

RAFIQ
(gentle sing-song)

There you are....

...Wake up...Wake up

Rafiq moves closer to the bed and grabs the sheets.

RAFIQ
(shouts)

Get up –

Rachel squirms to the middle of the bed; sheets clasped in her hands. She tries to cover herself. He grabs Rachel by the neckline of her t-shirt

RAFIQ

I said GET UP!

RACHEL

Rafiq…please.

Rafiq violently snatches Rachel out of the bed onto the floor. Rachel trying to catch her breath as Rafiq stands over her yelling.

RAFIQ

You are so stupid. Did you think I wouldn't find out? Look at you. I can't believe I married such a helpless, no good, useless woman -

Rachel doesn't move. SHE quietly sobs and this seems to enrage Rafiq more.

RAFIQ
(yelling)

Do you hear me talking to you?

Rachel doesn't respond. Rafiq grabs her by the arm and stands her up. Rachel does not make eye contact.

RAFIQ

I can't bear the sight of you anymore…You disgust me.

RACHEL

Baby, what did I do? What are you talking about?

RAFIQ

You know exactly what I'm talking about.

Takes an envelope out of his pocket, he throws it at her

RAFIQ

You've been cheating on me…Do you think I'm stupid Rachel..Huh You think I'm stupid?!

Rachel picks up the invitation and looks at it.

RACHEL

Rafiq, you don't understand. J is…

He snatches the invitation from her and rips it up. Rachel on her knees, tries to put the pieces back together.

RAFIQ

After all I've done for you. You know how many women wish they could stay home and not work? You know how many women would love to have a big house in the suburbs with a fine man like myself? You know how many women want to drive the latest Audi, get their hair and nails done every week, plus get an allowance to spend on whatever else they could possibly want?

RACHEL

Baby, I wouldn't dream of cheating on you.

RAFIQ

This is the thanks I get?

RACHEL

Rafiq. Can we please talk about this in a calm and rationale manner? Precious *is* sleeping.

RAFIQ

I am calm.

Silence. Rachel stands and tries to smooth things over.

_____

RACHEL

Rafiq, it's not what you think. If you would just let me explain.

RAFIQ

There's nothing to explain. I'm not good enough for you. I think you've made yourself clear. Now let me make myself clear. Until I decide otherwise, the only thing you will eat and drink are my directives. You will go where I tell you to go. You will speak only when spoken to and with whom I allow you to speak. You will perform your wifely duties – when and how I want it. In short, you will submit to me and me only…

RACHEL

Rafiq please. This is ridiculous. You can't…

Rafiq slaps Rachel. She falls onto the bed.

RAFIQ
(yells down at her)

Who do you think you are? Don't you ever tell me what I can and cannot do. This is my house.

Rachel rising from the bed angry.

RACHEL

You -

RAFIQ
(motions to slap Rachel)

Shut up

Precious enters as she reaches for her father's arm.

PRECIOUS
(yelling)

No daddy….Stop it….Please daddy.

Rafiq pushes her out of the way.

RAFIQ

Get off of me you little brat.

Precious runs to her mother's side crying. Rachel holds Precious.

RACHEL

You are out of control

Precious pushes her mother back into the bedroom. Rafiq tries to charge after them but Precious locks the door. He goes into another part of the house. Precious helps her mother to the bed. Precious kneels beside the bed and begins to pray. DANCER reappears and dances very sharp and forced movements, symbolic of turmoil.

PRECIOUS

Dear God, It's me again. I'm sure you're probably tired of me by now. But could you please help my mom and dad stop fighting. It's getting really bad. I am scared. I hate when this happens. I wish my dad was dead. No..no. I take that back. I just wish there was some way you could fix them. Make my mom strong and make my dad stop being so mean and yelling all the time. I know that somehow this is all my fault. I'm sorry God for being such a bad girl. But I promise, if you fix my parents, this one last time, I'll be good forever. Bless mom, dad, and me. I love you. Amen.

Familiar children's song in sad chords lights out.

SCENE TWO
THE PRESS

Lights reveal Amber and Patrick's living room. They are seated at their decorated dining room table. On the table are a glass of juice and a cup of coffee, utensils, and napkins. She wears a casual pant suite, he wears a pair of denim jeans and a button down shirt. Patrick picks up his coffee cup

PATRICK

You know service was really powerful last night. But it was strange. Worship ushered us right into the presence of the Holy Spirit and the word hit right where it was needed, but I noticed in talking with some of the saints afterward, that they heard the word but wasn't changed by it.

AMBER

Well, most people don't want to be accountable for the word. They want to shout over it. That's what we have been trained to do – believe that God is moved by the dance and shout. We feel that worship takes to long and requires us to give a whole lot for a seemingly small return.

PATRICK

But what's the shout about if you haven't been dealt with or spoken to in the midst of the worship. To me, it's the intimacy with God that brings about the praise and the shout. We praise because there's been a breakthrough – in our lives, our situations, and circumstances.

AMBER

Clearly the message talked about the steps that we needed
to take, as well as the state of mind that we needed to be in as
Christians, in order tap into the mysteries of God. But most
people dismiss the prerequisites and wait for the "You'll get
a car, a house, a mysterious check in the mail" part of the
sermon.

PATRICK

But you can't have a reward without hard work.

AMBER

Why not? We live in a society that tells us daily that for the
low, low bargain basement price of your soul, morals, values,
and character, that you can have whatever you want, no cash
down. So who needs Jesus?

PATRICK

I do.

AMBER

I know boo. That's why we always sit close to the altar.

*They share a laugh. Amber gets up from the table headed
to the kitchen..*

PATRICK

Yeah you better go fetch me my breakfast.

AMBER

Fruit Loops or Wheaties?

PATRICK

I'm going to check the machine dear. And when I get back, you better have my breakfast.

AMBER
(walks away)

Hot grits, comin' up!

Patrick chuckles as he goes to the machine. He pushes the button and it beeps.

ANSWERING MACHINE
(beep)

You have 3 messages.

MESSAGE 1 (JOY)

Hey girl. Didn't hear from you. Just wanted to make sure you got the invite. Call me if you didn't. Love you. Tell Pat I said Hey.

PATRICK
(mocking)

H-e-e-e-y

MESSAGE 2 (VOICEOVER)

Hello are you looking to refinance your home? Well have we got a deal for you. WWW & J Home Realty is right for you. Give us a call at 1-800-555-8855.

MESSAGE 3 (VOICEOVER)

Hello, Amber this is Dr. Roberts. Your test results have returned. There's no easy way to say this…Uh I need you to come to my office first thing on Monday.

Patrick hears plates crashing to the floor in the kitchen. Patrick runs to her side.

PATRICK

Are you all right? Baby, what's wrong?

Amber upset as Patrick sits her down and cleans up the mess while she speaks.

AMBER

Time and time again that prayer has been prayed. And when prayer, fasting, laying on of hands doesn't seem to help…it makes you question if God is real or if He's just some figment of your imagination that we've become obsessed with because everybody else says it's right. Maybe it's just not His will…I don't know anymore…I just …

Amber puts her head down and sighs heavily. Patrick returns to the table and comforts her. He lifts her head and looks into her eyes.

PATRICK
(supportive)

I still believe that we will have a child.

AMBER

I'm afraid you're going to have to believe for the both of us.

PATRICK

Oh come on baby, you can't give up now.

AMBER
(frustrated)

Why Not?!

PATRICK

Because what if it is His will? Then, we'll never know…

Amber interrupts, now yelling to make her point.

AMBER

How long Patrick? Huh? How long? How much longer?

PATRICK

Amber, calm down. We just have to be patient.

AMBER

Patrick, I am not getting any younger.

PATRICK

That's not an excuse. People are having kids at an older age everyday. Take Abraham and Sarah for example….

AMBER

Uh…We're in the middle of a discussion here, would you mind not joking

PATRICK

Fine. But my feelings haven't changed. I still believe

AMBER

You know, that's so easy for you to say because you don't have a clue as to what it's like.

Amber sucks her teeth.

AMBER

You, nor anybody else for that matter, understands the way I feel. I just wish God would hurry up. Because I'm getting really tired of waiting.

PATRICK

No good thing ever comes quickly. Listen, there are times when I want to throw in the towel and give up too, but I realize that I could be missing out on something big so each day I ask the Lord to give me another boost of strength, courage and patience.

AMBER

But Pat you don't know what it feels like seeing other women with their babies – at the mall buying all these cute little clothes, in the beauty parlor taking up space with their strollers, at the grocery store trying to hold the bottle and shop. Every time I see them, it just reminds me...of where I'm not and at this rate, where I may never be

Amber now begins to cry. Patrick moves closer to Amber and holds her in his arms.

PATRICK

We have to trust God's decision and whatever He decides, know that He and I will always be right by your side to love you and take care of you.

AMBER

I don't know what to do anymore. I feel like I'm losing control.

PATRICK

What we've been doing all along praying and believing that God would see us through. It has been prayer that has kept us these 5 years and God has been faithful and good to us. He won't fail us now or ever.

AMBER

But I can't help but feel like that's what He's done.

PATRICK

What?! How could you fix your mouth to say something ridiculous like that?

Patrick gently pulls her from him and looks her in the eyes.

PATRICK

Listen, God loves you. He has heard every one of your cries, seen every one of your tantrums, and listened to every one of your prayers. He's trying to teach us something. But we've got to be in the right position to hear from Him. Oh Baby

Patrick hugs his wife. He closes his eyes and begins to weep in praise.

PATRICK

Jesus….Jesus…Jesus I welcome you in this place. We glorify your name. We worship you. We magnify your name. We humble ourselves in your presence right now. Thank you Jesus. Hallelujah. Thank you Jesus. Father you said if we had faith as small as a mustard seed that you would honor it. So we ask that you would increase our faith right now. We desire your will to be done. And whatever the outcome, we trust that you will continue to guide us and grant us your wisdom. Where we lack understanding and insight, teach us to trust and to be patient with you while in our waiting season. We love you and we thank you for your many blessings. In Jesus Name. Amen.

Music underscores this action as lights fade.

SCENE THREE
BLING, BLING

Peaches is on her way to a cattle call audition. She is dressed in sunglasses, and an abnormally sophisticated outfit. Cell phone ringing. Peaches answers the phone.

PEACHES

Hello

AGENT

Hey Peaches, Just called to remind you about today's video shoot and to tell you the good news.

Peaches places her magazine aside.

PEACHES

I'm on my way as we speak. What's the good news?

AGENT

There's a new artist on the hip hop scene that's requesting you to audition next month for lead dancer in his upcoming music video and East Coast tour.

PEACHES

Are you serious? He wants me...Thank you. Thank you... Thank you. You're the best agent.

AGENT

Hey, it's you who make my job easy. Keep up the good work. Now here's the info: New York, Monday, May 15, 9AM, MTV Building.

PEACHES

Wait a sec…

Peaches reaches for a pen and her agenda book, located in her bag. Joy's invite falls to the ground. She picks it up, reads it over, checks the date, then

PEACHES

Ok, go ahead

AGENT

New York, Monday, May 15, 9AM, MTV Building. Ok?

PEACHES

Got it.

AGENT

Good luck today. I'll see you next month.

PEACHES

Thanks again. See ya

Peaches hangs up the phone and laughs aloud. She places the phone in the bag and pulls out a mirror to check herself before continuing.

PEACHES

God you are so awesome. Thank you for allowing me to look this good. I wouldn't trade my life for anything. From being broke in ballet to paid in hip hop...you definitely ordered the right steps for me.

Peaches begins walking toward the studio.
She opens the door to find several women who look exactly like herself.

ANNOUNCER

#114, #115, #116

Peaches signs in and obtains a number. She goes to sit among the other dancers, who are staring her up and down, but decides She will go to the bathroom instead. She is seated in the stall, feeling somewhat insecure. She reaches for the cross around her neck and kisses it. She closes her eyes.

ALTER EGO

Stop kidding yourself…that cross lost its meaning when you signed on the dotted line.

PEACHES

Ballet was taking me nowhere. God knows that -

ALTER EGO

And so what? Life in the fast lane is taking you places?

PEACHES

I have been to more places than most people my age

ALTER EGO

At what cost?

PEACHES

Whatever!

ALTER EGO

Face it! You're a disgrace!

PEACHES

Everybody's proud of me.

ALTER EGO

Yeah right.

PEACHES

Look, I did what I thought was best for me.

ALTER EGO

All you think about is yourself.

PEACHES

Who else is there? Look I'm not the church type anymore –
that's my past. I'm happier now than I've ever been.

ALTER EGO

You're far from it. When are you going to wake up and
quit playing this game with yourself? You think because you
are 27, have a penthouse on the west coast, a chauffer, drink
champagne with dinner, and wear designer clothes, that you're
somebody. And what happens when it's all gone. It wasn't
always like this, and it won't always be like this either.

PEACHES

People just hatin' on me. While they're waiting on God,
I'm making it happen.

ANNOUNCER
(in the background)

Number 148...149...

Peaches looks up to the ceiling.

PEACHES

Look, I know you're disappointed in me. I just can't seem to get things right. And I know it's wrong but I love the attention and all this fancy stuff. I don't want to be with you if I can't have it all. And I'm not ready to give it ALL up...I'm just not ready. So just stop pressuring me. I'll let you know when and if I'm ready.

Peaches walks out of the bathroom.

ANNOUNCER

Number 150

Peaches confidently walks out of the bathroom and into the studio. She takes her coat off to reveal an eye catching outfit. She and other Girls take their position to perform. Loud hip hop music. Peaches and other Girls perform an electrifying, gyrating, routine similar to a secular music video. Lights out.

SCENE FOUR
THE MASK

JOY in the dance studio preparing for her rehearsal. She stretches throughout.

JOY

Well Lord, it's just you and me again. Better warm up

She stops stretching, and now sits on the floor.

I have an idea.

She jumps up.

Lord, Lemme holla at you for a minute. What if you, like Adam, took one of my ribs and made me a man. I could lie down right here and when I get up, **He-ca-ma-sah** - My boo is standing right in front of me.

She speaks to this imaginary man as though he were really standing there.

Umph, Umph, Umph, with your fine self.

She shakes her head and giggles.

Truth be told, if he were really standing here, I'd probably pass out and on my way to the floor knock myself unconscious thereby not being able to enjoy my blessing. Oh well, so much for that idea.

She continues stretching on the floor.

I was wondering: Why are singles told to read all these books on: "How to enjoy being single"; "Practicing purity"; "Being a woman of excellence"; "How to wait for Mr. Right". *(upset)*
I can't meet Mr. Wrong. I've had it. Lord, I don't think I can take much more of this.

Tears are streaming down her face.

I've prayed, I've fasted, I've tithed, I've gotten in ministry, I've attended the singles gala, parties, picnics, fellowships, all of which were overly populated by females and further complicated by the competition over the same two male attendees. I've done everything you wanted me to do. Why can't you do what I want you to do for me? Why are you punishing me? I've got the degrees, I've got the house, I've got the car, I've got great friends, and a loving family, but there's still that longing *(slowly, taking her time as if really being caressed in this moment)* to be held, to be thought about, to be needed and wanted by …I hate being single.

Looking up and pointing at God

Do you hear me Lord?

Screaming

I hate it.

Distraught

You promised you'd supply all my needs. ALL of them.

She sobs

Tell me why, Lord, if I'm so fearfully and wonderfully made, then how come they don't notice me.
What's wrong with me? Why must I be separated - set apart? Why must I be different? Why me? Huh? Huh! *(tough)* Well I've got news for you: I don't want to be different anymore...I want to be like everyone else whose livin' it up -

Joy feels guilty. She slides down the wall onto the floor and cries. Then after several moments, she stops crying, clears her throat and calms herself. She wipes her tears.

Joy, you promised not to do this to yourself anymore. Pull yourself together, girl. Get up and shake it off.

She slowly stands to her feet and shakes herself with confidence and speaks boldly.

Satan you are a LIAR. And I will not go crazy this day. Greater is He that is in me, than he that is in the world. God has a plan for me and I will not compromise. It's not easy, but I'm going to wait. You almost had me...but almost isn't good enough. You've got to do better than that, because I serve an awesome God and He won't let me go out like that. You CAN'T have my mind. You CAN'T have my peace. I've come too far...

Joy takes a moment to praise God.

Thank you Jesus....Ooo God I thank you for being so good to me...for loving me even when I talk straight junk...I sho nuff couldn't be you because if I was listening to me, a lightening bolt would have just struck the minute I thought about going off the deep end.

JOY takes a deep breath and looks at her watch. She reaches for her cell phone in her bag – the invitation falls out. She picks up the invitation and sits on the floor.

I can't wait to see the girls next month...It's been five years since we've last seen each other. We have so much to catch up on.

Joy smiles at the invitation and reads aloud.

It's been too long since we've last met. I miss you. Come and steal away with me for a weekend of fun, laughter, and intimacy. Can't wait to see you, J

She makes a call on her cell phone when Michael enters.

JOY

I was just about to call you.

Michael walks over and kisses Joy on the cheek and hugs her.

MICHAEL

Sorry I'm late.

JOY

It's cool.

Michael reaches out his hand for Joy.

MICHAEL

Ready for our début

JOY

I'm little nervous.

MICHAEL

Why, you're a great dancer. Don't worry, it will be off the hook.

JOY

I just don't want to mess up. Plus my best friends will be there and Pastor and -

MICHAEL

Maybe you'll feel better if we rehearse.

JOY
(smiling)

Yeah.

Joy and Michale take their position. Lights fade.

Patrons will hear a flight announcement followed by a conversation being held by JOY, AMBER, PEACHES, and RACHEL.

FLIGHT ANNOUNCEMENT

Flight number 301 is now arriving at gate one. We'd like to take this opportunity to thank you for flying Psalms Airline. We hope each of you reaches your next destination safely.

PEACHES (VOICEOVER)

I'm here

RACHEL (VOICEOVER)

Peaches you haven't changed a bit, with your crazy self.

AMBER (VOICEOVER)

Joy, look at you miss thing. You are looking radiant. Is there someone in your life?

RACHEL/PEACHES (VOICEOVER)

Okay Joy, spill it….

JOY (VOICEOVER)

Yall are so stupid….I'm not seeing anyone.

PEACHES (VOICEOVER)

She's lying.

JOY (VOICEOVER)

Okay, can we please get off of me and let's get this party started. I've missed you guys...

ACT TWO

SCENE ONE
I GOT ALL MY SISTA'S WIT' ME

Joy enters the dance studio, which is nicely decorated with pictures. In the center are an area rug and 4 extra large pillows assembled in a circle for the girls to sit. Joy waits for friends. Rachel, Amber, Peaches enter the dance studio struggling with their bags. Once in the studio, They begin strangely looking around. Rachel, Amber, Joy each dressed comfortably and casually. Rachel has a cardigan, which she does not take off. Peaches wears jeans which are shoestring tied up both legs, a shirt which covers the front but ties across the back, stiletto boots, sunglasses, weave and heavy make up. Amber is wearing a two piece pants suit. Joy is wearing a cute 2 piece sweat suite.

PEACHES

Uh, most people who are invited to spend a weekend with someone are taken to the hosts home so that they can rest and freshen up from their trip.

RACHEL

Yeah, why exactly are we at a dance studio?

AMBER

Joy is there something you want to tell us?

JOY
(jokingly)

Surprise!

They do not look amused and are still standing next to their bag. Peaches gathers her things to leave.

JOY

Oh calm down. I know it's somewhat of an inconvenience. I just thought it would be nice to recreate the moment where we first met -- but if you'd rather go to the apartment then...

AMBER
(looking sternly at Peaches)

We're not going anywhere. *(coaxing)* Guys come on, let's not get off on the wrong foot. We're here to have fun.

RACHEL
(hugging Joy)

We was just playing girl....

PEACHES
(jokingly)

Sike.

They all laugh and begin discussing Peaches' arrival at the airport.

RACHEL

In your defense Peaches, I can understand why you are tired.
Why with all your fans running to greet you at the airport...the
autographs, pictures, and free thrills, who can bear to stand...

PEACHES

Joy, I think we're going to need a glass of Haterade over
here.

Rachel runs over to Peaches and hands her a piece of
paper.

RACHEL
(mockingly)

Can I have your autograph?

AMBER
(begging)

Me too..Me too.

Peaches holds her hand up encouraging the girls to wait.

PEACHES

Okay guys. One at a time

Peaches signs her name on the piece of paper and hands it back to Rachel.

RACHEL
(laughing)

You are such a good dancer. I want to be just like you when I grow up.

PEACHES

Well that should take a minute, so I don't have to worry about any competition from you.

Rachel holds her hand up and rolls her eyes.

RACHEL

Whateva'

PEACHES
(smiles at Rachel)

Jealousy isn't a cute color on you…

Rachel gives Peaches the evil eye. Amber interrupts their moment.

AMBER

No, but what about that guy that smacked you on the behind and asked for your number.

JOY
(as if daydreaming)

Oh Amber, some of us can only dream about getting that kind of attention.

AMBER

You have got to be kidding me…

JOY
(surprised)

What?!

Amber looks at Joy.

AMBER

I'm not even going to entertain your foolishness today Joy.

Amber turns her back to Joy and looks at Peaches. Joy sucks her teeth and goes to prepare lunch.

AMBER

Tamara

PEACHES

It's Peaches

AMBER

Peaches..Tamara. Whatever your name is. I can't believe you would allow anyone to disrespect you like that.

RACHEL
(with attitude)

What do you expect, she's a hoochie!

PEACHES

I am not a hoochie. I am a professional music dancer. You're just mad because –

AMBER, RACHEL

You're beautiful, we know…

Both bust out laughing. Joy enters with the food and brings it to the circle of pillows.

JOY

Ladies, lunch is served.

Rachel, Peaches, and Amber get comfortable on their pillows.

JOY

Who would like to say grace?

AMBER

I'll do the honors

RACHEL

I'm hungry, so try not to make this a sermon

AMBER

Shut up and bow your heads

They each takes one another's hand. Peaches makes a cat sound. Rachel laughs. Amber squeezes Rachel's hand.

RACHEL

Ouch, stop squeezing my hand.

JOY

Uh, the food is getting cold

AMBER

Shh!! *(she prays)* Gracious Father we thank you for this opportunity to share in fellowship. We ask that you would bless this food and the hands that prepared it as we eat for the nourishment of our bodies. We thank you in Jesus name. Amen.

ALL

Amen

The women begin serving as they reminisce about the 'good ole college days' and the dance classes they took together.

AMBER

You know who I ran into at the mall the other day, Ms. Studimier

RACHEL

Dag. That brings back memories. That's where we all met, Intro to Dance: Ballet 1. Remember our first day of class.

JOY

How could any of us forget that?

RACHEL

I remember the look on Ms. Studimier's face when Tamara came in *(laughing)*. It was like "help me...somebody please help me".

AMBER

Yeah, I knew back then that Tamara was gonna be somebody

PEACHES
(smiling)

How? Did you notice something special about me?

AMBER
(trying to hold her laughter)

Yeah, that tacky behind bright red and glitter leotard you had on.

All laugh.

AMBER

Girl, the fashion police should have locked you up.

AMBER

You guys are just jealous because she took a special interest in me.

JOY

That's because you required special help.

RACHEL

Not much has changed...

Peaches looks at Rachel

PEACHES

A whole lot has changed. Thank you very much.

AMBER

Those were the days.

JOY

Do you remember that night after the winter recital?

RACHEL

When Ms. Studimier had the class over for warm cookies, and hot chocolate with marshmallows.

JOY

We were sitting around the fireplace listening to Ms. Studimier tell us about her days on Broadway and how God opened so many doors and granted so many opportunities to share her gift with so many great and influential people.

AMBER

She was a legend of her time and many took her for granted. She was famous but so humble. She always encouraged us to trust God with everything…even our biggest dreams.

RACHEL

I remember tears streaming down my face as she shared her testimony…Her favorite scripture…

PEACHES

I remember her praying for me

RACHEL
(joking)

Well somebody had to…

PEACHES
(offended)

You know, you guys always thought that you were so much better than me. Just because I'm not some Ms. Goody Two Shoes -

JOY

That's not true.

PEACHES

Well at least one of you is being honest with themselves.

JOY

What's that supposed to mean?

Peaches looks at Joy

PEACHES
(with an attitude)

You're just as much of an actress as I am Joy.*(pointing at Rachel and Amber)* You may be foolin' them, but you don't fool me.

Joy puts her fork down and stares furiously into Peaches face.

JOY

How dare you judge me.

PEACHES

Get off your spirit filled horse and stop pretending your life is so perfect.

Rachel and Amber look at one another. Amber interrupts

JOY

I hope you're listening to yourself Ms. Superstar.

AMBER

Okay ladies, that's enough. Calm down so we can finish our lunch

PEACHES/JOY
(looking at her)

Stay out of this Amber.

PEACHES

This conversation is long overdue. Truth be told, the only reason our lives look different is because you have Jesus and I have make-up.

There is a long silence. Amber and Rachel sit quietly and shake their heads in dismay. Every now and then, they cut each other a glance.

JOY

I never said I was perfect.

PEACHES

Looks can be deceiving, can't they Joy

JOY

You want to hear the truth…uh..is that what you are after?

PEACHES
(sarcastic)

It's the only way you can be set free.

JOY

I am and have always been jealous of you, your beauty, your relationships, your carefree life. So after all these years, you were right. Are you happy now?

RACHEL

What?! Joy, you can't be serious. Peaches is hardly the person you want to be a role model.

AMBER
(under her breath)

You got that right.

Peaches gives Rachel and Amber a dirty look. Joy looks at Peaches

JOY

But she has it all.

RACHEL

No she doesn't. She's missing the most important thing…
Listen Joy, you have got to want more than a couple of one
night stands.

JOY

Well at least she's having sex.

AMBER

It's not all that you think it is…

RACHEL

Actually Joy, sex is so overrated.

Peaches looks down.

PEACHES

They're right, Joy…you deserve better.

Peaches sighs and sits quietly with her head down.

AMBER
(nurturing)

And so do you Peaches

RACHEL

You guys just have to wait and trust that God will bring you someone that will compliment your lives - not add more drama to them.

PEACHES

Drama is right! Joy that's why you should keep your eyes on the men at church, work, and school.

JOY

Oh yeah. I can take my pick from the crem de la crem: old and gray, self centered, unemployed and living with their momma, or just plain ole, I'm not interested.

AMBER

Stop looking. Just find yourself doing what God's called you to do and he'll come along soon enough.

Joy sucks her teeth and rolls her eyes.

JOY

Yes mom

They all share a laugh.

RACHEL

Yall better enjoy being single while you can. And Peaches, you're not a lost cause.

AMBER

That's right. God can still use you in spite of that mess you call dancing.

RACHEL

He can change you into a graceful swan just like me.

AMBER

Is that what you call yourself?

PEACHES

You're more like a duck. Quack. Quack

Peaches laughs in Rachel's face.

JOY

Ooo, that wasn't even right girl. You gonna let them play you like that?

PEACHES

Joy, why you always trying to start something?

RACHEL

What's the matter Peaches, you scurred?

PEACHES
(ghetto)

Now Rachel you know that was a dumb question. I can beat you any day and any time

Rachel gets up from the circle and steps to Peaches. She is now standing over Peaches.

RACHEL

Now is as good a time as any..let's roll

Peaches stands up. Both are now standing eye to eye. Amber stands and separates the two of them. Peaches, Amber, and Rachel walk over to empty floor space in the dance studio.

AMBER
(announcer voice)

Ladies and gentlemen, in the left corner of the ring...
weighing in at 200lbs, Rachel the Raging Rose Petal

Rachel looks at Amber with a perplexed look and then looks at Peaches. Peaches laughs. Rachel begins shadow boxing.

AMBER
(announcer voice)

In the right corner of the ring, weighing in at 89lbs, Tamara the Tenacious Tulip

Peaches looks up at Amber. Rachel laughing, Amber shrugs her shoulder and throws her hands up. She begins to laugh. Peaches now shadow boxing.

AMBER

Come together.

Peaches and Rachel come together in the center of the dance studio.

AMBER cont.

Fight nice

Rachel and Peaches give each other a pound and back into their respective corners.

AMBER

Ding, Ding, Ding

Joy steps in between them.

JOY

Why don't we take this challenge to the dance floor.

PEACHES

Why don't you stay out of this?

AMBER

Although watching the two of you beat each other's brains out would be quite entertaining, I agree with Joy. We may see some fancier footwork on the dance floor.

RACHEL

Thanks Amber for

PEACHES

interrupting your butt whoopin'

RACHEL
(at Peaches)

I was playing in the first place but you always have to take stuff out of proportion

JOY

Are we gonna dance or what?

PEACHES

Yall might as well pay up, because I'm going to win this challenge.

JOY
(laughing)

On what? A wing and a prayer?

PEACHES

Okay Joy, let's see what you got then.

While talking, Joy begins walking. She picks up a chair from the corner of the studio and brings it to the center of the dance studio.

JOY
(like a preacher)

See, Unlike the heathens. This is what saved…sanctified.. filled with the Holy Ghost, Fire Baptised, Holy, God fearing women of God do….Heeyy. This dance is only for those who love and serve the Lord.

PEACHES

Whateva Joy. I love the Lord. He knows my heart. Besides, it don't take all that. See, so you the one missing out, because I can love Him, and still make a phat living…

Peaches snaps her finger and rolls her neck at Joy.

AMBER

That child is brainwashed for sure…

JOY

Just pay attention Peaches, because when you finally surrender, you're gonna have a lot to shout about.

Joy takes her chair and turns it so the back of it is facing her. She places one hand on the chair. Shouting music begins, Joy goes forth in a shout. A few minutes later, they all jump up and begin clapping and stomping their feet to the beat.

AMBER
(looking at the other girls)

Now that's my kinda dancin'

Joy finishes by faking a faint. Rachel runs to grab her and places her gently on the floor. Amber begins to fan and Peaches stands over Joy shaking her head in disbelief.

RACHEL
(singing)

Have your way...Have your way...

AMBER

Yes Lawd

Joy on the floor motioning as if being delivered

RACHEL
(now caught up in the song)

I said...Have your way..Oooo Have your way. Lawd Jesus,
Have your way.

Joy sits up. They now stare at Rachel.
Rachel notices the silence and looks at the girls.

JOY

Well, now that the Spirit packed up and left...

PEACHES

There goes her deliverance and we know she needed it...
Dag Rachel, some kinda help you are.

AMBER

I know...most people usher the Spirit in...

PEACHES
(demonstrating)

Instead, you've got him hiding, peaking to see if its safe to
come out again.

RACHEL

I KNOW, yall not talking about my singing.

JOY

No, if it was singing, we would call it that.

They all share a laugh. Joy stands to her feet and looks at Peaches.

JOY

I believe the floor now belongs to you

Joy takes her hand and motions it towards the center of their now half circle.

AMBER
(to herself)

I can't wait to see this one

Peaches walking to the coat rack, looks over her shoulder at Amber.

PEACHES

I heard that

Peaches takes a tape out of her pocketbook and proceeds to the stereo. She pops in a tape and returns to the half circle. Stereo blasts version of "Work It" by Missy Elliott Peaches begins gyrating and swinging her body parts across the stage. When she completes her routine, She looks at the girls with a wide smile and excitement. Their mouths are wide open and eyes bucked.

AMBER
(shocked)

Goodness gracious girl. Have you no shame?!

RACHEL

And, this is what you do for a living

Joy gives Rachel a dirty look then looks at Peaches.

JOY

She's an entertainer, what did you expect?

AMBER

Not that

There is a slight pause. Joy looks at Amber

JOY

Well let's see, what you have to offer Amber

Amber looks at Peaches

AMBER

Definitely something more classy and tasteful than that.

Peaches sighs loudly and sucks her teeth.

AMBER

Joy, do you still have that tap board?

JOY

Yup

Amber gets up and goes to the stereo while Joy and Rachel get the board. They place the board in the middle of the half circle. Amber has a pair of tap shoes in her bag. She places them on her feet and with a large smile walks over to the tap board. She takes her place. As an upbeat gospel jazz selection plays. Amber happily taps while the others look on.

PEACHES

Why in the world is she cheesin like that?

RACHEL

For the same reason, you were carryin' on...none of yall have any sense.

JOY

She's just happy

PEACHES

More like her bones are probably cracking and rather than cry, she has her permanent *(demonstrating)* 'I'm in Pain' grin

RACHEL
(laughs)

Shut up. I'm gonna tell her what yall said about her

JOY

I recall you saying she didn't have any sense.

Rachel gets quiet. Amber is done, She extends her arms wide open towards the girls.

AMBER

Ta Da

PEACHES

Somebody throw that girl a quarter

JOY

You are funny Amber

AMBER

Oh yall got jokes

Amber walks confidently back to her seat and ignores the girl's comments.

PEACHES

Okay Rachel, it's your turn. Now don't get too deep on us now.

AMBER

You know it takes us forever to figure out what the dance is all about anyway

RACHEL

Watch and learn.

Rachel takes off her cardigan. They immediately notice the bruises on her arm and back however they say nothing. Rachel goes to the stereo and places her tape in. A version of "Still I Rise" by Yolanda Adams begins. Rachel dances a dance of pain, isolation, and fear yet finding peace and freedom in the end. She cries upon completing the dance. The others come to Rachel's side and embraces her. Lights out.

SCENE TWO
LEAN ON ME/HEALING BALM

All the women are sitting in different postures listening to and confronting one another as They share their stories.

RACHEL

I don't know what to do anymore

PEACHES

Personally, I would beat that no good niggah upside his head.

RACHEL

I mean, the fist time he hit me, I ignored it and made excuses for him, said he didn't mean it. I knew there was a lot going on at the job. So if it was a money thing, then I thought, maybe I should go back to work. But that wasn't it.

AMBER

How long has this been going on?

RACHEL

Well...since...since college.

JOY

Since college?! You were always so happy and all over each other.

RACHEL

That was in public.

AMBER

We only went by what you said and what we saw.

RACHEL

He didn't start hitting me until recently.

AMBER

There's no excuse. You shouldn't have to deal with any kind of abuse, physical or otherwise.

PEACHES

So help me understand why exactly you married him.

RACHEL

I got pregnant and I promised myself that I would never have a child out of wedlock. Rafiq was a star athlete and on the Dean's list in the School of Business. We were worried about our reputations, so we decided to get married, for both our sakes. It was a choice…and underneath all the negative stuff we really did love one another.

JOY

How come you never talked to us about this?

RACHEL

I didn't want you to worry about me besides you had your own lives to deal with.

AMBER

You didn't have to live with this by yourself. You should have called one of us.

JOY

What else are friends for, but go through with you, talk to or listen to, and share with…

RACHEL

I told Rafiq that if we were going to make it work that we would have to sit under a good ministry and get the word in us. Well he didn't want to hear any of that church stuff. But it wasn't an option for me, I had a child coming into the world.

PEACHES

So you did what you had to do?

RACHEL

I know that you don't understand.

JOY

No, I don't understand

RACHEL

And sometimes...neither do I.

AMBER

I know what you mean

RACHEL

Each day I ask God for strength. Even though my body, heart and mind doesn't seem like it can take much more...

PEACHES

Then take your stuff and be out, girl!!

RACHEL

It's not that simple

JOY

Why Rachel?

RACHEL

Because I believe in the covenant I made to God - "For better or for worse" I also have a child. I have to consider how it will effect her.

JOY

What about the effect it's having on her now?

Joy pauses to think and then looks at Rachel

JOY

Where is Precious anyway?

RACHEL

I scheduled a doctor's appointment for Precious so that he would leave me the car. I dropped her off at my mom's and drove up to be with you guys.

PEACHES

Girl, I'm surprised he didn't put out an APB on that car and send the SWAT team to comb the area looking for you.

They all chuckle.

RACHEL

While I was at the doctor's office, I wrote him a letter. We swung back past the house, I dropped it off and continued on my journey.

JOY

You're brave.

RACHEL

Despite everything, I'm still blessed and I trust that He will indeed bring us through.

AMBER

I admire your ability to trust despite the pain. I only wish
that I could.

RACHEL

You can and I'll stand with you if you need me to.

AMBER
(discouraged)

I appreciate it Rachel but I'm tired of…

RACHEL
(completing her thought)

Waiting. Me too, but the Bible says 'Wait on the Lord. Be
of good courage. He shall strengthen your heart.'

AMBER

I don't -

RACHEL

It's not about what you want. It's not even about you – It's
not about any of us.

AMBER

You don't see what I see

JOY

Whose eyes are you looking through? With Christ, all things are possible.

PEACHES

Didn't Patrick know before you were married, there was a possibility you couldn't have children?

AMBER
(softly)

Yes.

JOY

Then he wouldn't have married you if he didn't love you and wasn't happy with you, the way you are.

Amber begins to cry.

JOY

Amber I look up to you and Patrick's marriage because the love is real.

RACHEL

Enjoy what you and Patrick have in each other. I believe that God has so much more in store for our marriages. We can't allow this test to make us miss out on what God has for us.

Amber stops crying.

AMBER
(wiping tears and composing herself)

I guess this is why we needed to be here.

RACHEL

God set us up!!

They each take a moment to reflect and they each seem to finish each other's thoughts.

AMBER

Our struggles are different but the agony of wanting something so bad and feeling as though the prayers have fallen on deaf ear….

Rachel reaches over and gently rubs Amber's hands in comfort.

RACHEL

But knowing within your heart that they haven't….

JOY

Because you've said yes to His will and you know that where you are is where He wants you to be for right now

PEACHES

But what if you're running away from His will?

AMBER

You'll get tired and surrender.

JOY

Saying yes is the easy part; living out the yes is another story.

RACHEL

Tamara it's a process and until you finish the process

AMBER

He'll keep you right there…

JOY

Yet the awesome thing about God is his keeping you there is not for punishment but for refinement...

RACHEL

And it doesn't always feel good, and you don't always understand why, and at times you want to throw in the towel, but when He's done with you, you've got everything you need to fight your next battle.

AMBER

Peaches, believe me when I say, none of us are perfect; there are moments when we pass the tests and there are others when we fail. You just have to take each day as it comes.

JOY

Peaches, we've all back-slid or been disobedient at some point or another...But God forgives us and has mercy on us. It's never to late to say I'm sorry, I was wrong...or whatever you need to tell Him. Anytime is a good time, when you need to speak with God.

PEACHES

That's probably why I had to be here. This is a part of my process and I guess I need to make some choices.

AMBER

Well, there's no time like the present.

PEACHES

I don't know if I'm ready give up (stresses) everything. My life is a dream come true

RACHEL

And if you don't make the right choice, it can become a nightmare.

JOY

You'll never be ready. You'll never have it all together. You'll never have it all figured out.

RACHEL

But, if it's your desire to come back to Him and you feel Him tugging at you, just say yes. He'll take you right now where you are, just as you are.

PEACHES

He can't want me after all that I've done. The sex, the drugs, the money, the lying, the fighting – It's too much for Him to love me and want me.

AMBER

Peaches, no one sin is greater than another. Sin is sin. And God never stopped loving you. He's been there from the beginning. He knew you would go this way and now He's saying, I am the way.

RACHEL

And the choice will always be yours.

Peaches is crying and seeks the comfort of her friends. Rachel, Amber, and Joy surround Peaches.

JOY
(whispers)

Let's pray.

Rachel, Amber, and Tamara nod in agreement. They begin to worship, praise, speak in tongues. Peaches begins to cry and walks away from the other girls. She gets on her knees with her face to the floor and begins to repent.

PEACHES

God, I don't even know where to begin except thank you. Thank you for not throwing me away like the trash that I am. I'm sorry Lord...I was wrong to turn my back on you and think that I could do it all by myself....Oh God, I'm sorry for everything I've done; for all the embarrassments and disappointments Please take me back. I want to make things right. Please God take me back. I want to come back and live right...

AMBER

Hallelujah Jesus.

JOY

Yes God

RACHEL
(speaking in tongues)

Have your way...Thank you Jesus

PEACHES
(stretching out her arms)

Help me...Help me...Oh God wash me...I'm so filthy. I need you...I need you in my life. I can't make it without you.

The others continue to intercede and speak in tongues for Tamara.

PEACHES

You are my Savior. I give you full control. I say *(screaming)* Yes...Yes Lord...Yes. Whatever you want me to do....I say yes.

They all rejoice over Tamara's salvation. Tamara remains on the floor receiving all of her deliverance. Joy goes over to comfort Tamara and begins to pray. Prayers are done in a tag team form as if it were Spirit led. Mood Music plays underneath.

JOY
(leading the prayer)

Hallelujah...Hallelujah Jesus. Oh God we thank you for the spirit of brokenness right now. Thank you that our hearts have been made tender towards you. We thank you because we are positioned in the place where you desire us to be. Now God, speak to our hearts, our minds, our circumstances, the wounded places of our souls. We need to hear from you today

AMBER

We glorify you. We worship you with the fruit of our lips on today. We thank you for a renewed mind. Thank you for the transformation that is taking place. Thank you for restoration. We say yes...Yes to your will and Yes to your way. We surrender and submit to your will today. We will bless your name at all times- when we get and when we don't get; when things go our way and when you have your way, when we see our way out, and when we see no way out. We know our help comes from you.

RACHEL

So today God, we cast each and every care, every anxiety, every fear, every weight, every frustration, every disappointment, everything that's not according to your will, we leave it at the altar on today. God you know what we stand in need of. For you are a God who is able to do exceedingly, abundantly, above all that we ask or think. We declare today that there is no weapon formed against us that shall prosper. Satan you are a liar. Take your hands off our marriages. Take your hand off our children, Take your hand off our minds for you can not win. For we are victorious on today. Hallelujah

JOY

We bind every plan, trick and scheme of the enemy today. God you said in your word, that whatever we bound on earth, would be bound in heaven. And whatever we loosed on earth would be loosed in heaven. We plead the blood of Jesus.....

RACHEL

The blood of Jesus covers us...It covers our families....It covers our home, it covers our dance. In the name of Jesus. We are healed. We are delivered . We are set free on today.

Tamara stands to her feet and joins in the prayer and worship experience.

TAMARA

We thank you God that we no longer walk in darkness. But we walk in your truth. You have set before us, life and death. We chose life on today God.

AMBER

We declare that we have your peace, your joy, your wisdom, your patience. We thank you for your Grace and Mercy towards us. We trust in you today. We believe that you have heard our prayer. And we stand in agreement...

All the women join hands as prayer comes to a close.

JOY

We thank you that every good and perfect gift comes from you. Perfect our gifts on today...Use us for your glory. And we'll be so careful to give your name all the glory, all the honor, and all the praise that you, and you alone are worthy of. We bless your name Jesus....

As they continue to worship God a version of worship music comes in to saturate the atmosphere.

RACHEL

We worship you, O God. You are so holy Lord.

AMBER

Excellent is thy name in all the earth.

TAMARA

Thank you Jesus. Thank you Jesus.

JOY

Hallelujah. Hallelujah...Hallelujah.

The four friends form a circle as a symbol of unity and accountability and begin an African-like dance (no African music) which tells a story of their exile from captivity to freedom and deliverance. Mood Music

Each will dance a presentation of their personal deliverance from: Joy: insecurity/loneliness to confidence/ satisfaction with Christ. Tamara: world/loneliness to salvation and freedom. Rachel: domestic violence and fear to courage and trust. Amber: hopelessness/faithless to contentment and obedience

They return to the circle and share the fruits of their transformation: strength, healing, power, freedom, love, peace, intimacy - in the dance. Lights out.

SCENE THREE
DANCE WITH ME

Lights reveal before service in the fellowship hall. Michael is dressed for church performance. He looks at his watch.

MICHAEL

Where are you Joy? Church starts in 45 minutes.

Michael begins pacing the floor and sighing heavily.

MICHAEL

Relax man. You get like this every time you see her. Lord, I've never felt this way about a woman before and I can't really read how she feels about me. So could you send me a sign, please.

Joy rushes in dressed beautifully.

JOY
(hugging Michael)

Sorry I'm late.

Michael enjoys the embrace.

MICHAEL

It's okay. We have plenty of time.

Joy is all nerves. Michael tries to calm Joy.

MICHAEL
(looking into her eyes)

Joy, we'll be fine.

JOY

I know...*(sigh)* It's just.

Michael gently grabs her hand.

MICHAEL

Let's pray.

Joy bows her head.

MICHAEL

Father we thank you for the art of dance. We thank you for using us as vessels to deliver your word through the arts. As we use our gifts, may it bring you glory and honor. We ask that the Holy Spirit dance in and through us so that someone's life might be changed. We ask these things in your holy and most wonderful name. Amen.

JOY

Amen....You better pray...Umph

Joy gives Michael a look. Michael is excited but remains cool. Joy and Michael take their positions. As a Love Ballad begins. Joy and Michael dance. It is apparent through the dance that Michael is interested in Joy. When the dance is over, Michael and Joy return to the fellowship hall.

MICHAEL

I felt like I was dancing on air.

JOY

I think that was our best yet.

Rachel, Amber, and Tamara enter with compliments.

RACHEL

That was so...

AMBER
(finishing the sentence)

Beautiful...You two make a good couple

Joy looks at Amber

AMBER cont.
(corrects herself)

...of dancers. You make a great couple of dancers.

RACHEL
(snickering)

He is perfect

TAMARA

I know that's right

RACHEL

Stop it you two

TAMARA

Well if she don't' jump on him, I will.

JOY

You'll have to excuse my fiends.

Joy looks at the girls and rolls her eyes. She introduces each to Michael.

TAMARA

Okay hate to interrupt the introductions but I'm hungry.

AMBER

Me too.

RACHEL

Will you two be joining us?

JOY
(smiling)

Michael, would you like to join us?

MICHAEL

I'd love to but I know this is your special weekend together so I'll decline. *(to Joy)* Give you a call later?

The others make faces at one another.

JOY
(girlish)

Yeah…

MICHAEL

Nice meeting you ladies.

He exits.

AMBER, RACHEL, PEACHES

You too…

AMBER
(teasing)

Looks like somebody's got the hots for you…

Joy blushes. Lights out.

SCENE FOUR
MY SISTER, MY FRIEND

Lights reveal Joy on the couch. The doorbell rings. Joy answers the door. It's Tamara who enters hysterical and plops on the couch. Joy upon sitting hands her a tissue from the box on the table.

JOY

What's wrong? What happened?

TAMARA

Remember the audition I told you about.

JOY

Uh

TAMARA

The one I showed you the other day

JOY

Uh Huh

TAMARA

Well, it was today.

JOY

How did it go?

TAMARA
(hysterical)

How did it go..How did it go. It was ***awful***.

JOY

Well, Tell me what happened?

TAMARA

They dismissed me before I could even finish.

JOY

What?!

TAMARA

They said 'You're not exactly the type we're looking for' in a real nasty and sarcastic tone.

JOY

Did you audition with the same routine you showed us?

TAMARA

Yeah. Why?

JOY

No wonder.

Joy tries not to laugh but can't help it.

TAMARA

This isn't funny Joy. We're talking about my career here. Things were supposed to get better once I came back to Christ

JOY

Who told you that...Tamara, when you said yes, you said yes to everything that God has in store for you *(pause)* Some things you're going to have to let go.

TAMARA

Dancing pays the bills.

JOY

No one said you had to stop dancing. Just change -

TAMARA

Ballet can't pay my bills

JOY

It can when God is the choreographer.

TAMARA

I don't want to hear that right now. I have to think realistically.

Joy continues.

JOY

It was God who gave you the ability to dance in the first place. So when you said yes, you gave the dance back to Him. Trust…He will direct you.

TAMARA

Aaaugh. I can't believe this. Why does this have to be so difficult? See this is why so many people stay in the world.

JOY

Why because you can't have control?

TAMARA

Exactly. I gave up everything to get nothing.

JOY

Tell me you don't really believe that.

TAMARA

It feels like that...

Tamara puts her head down. Joy picks Tamara's head up and stares her in the eyes

JOY

Tamara you gave up your will for His plan. And just like God allowed you to dance for the world, He will give you a dance that will glorify Him and draw people in to the kingdom of God. After we finished praying the other night, God reminded me of Ms. Studimier's favorite dance scripture, Psalm 30:11 (Amp) 'You have turned my mourning into dancing for me; You have put off my sackcloth and girded me with gladness'. Tamara, that's what God has done for each of us. He's removed the burden and replaced it with His joy, His peace. It's going to take some time but let the Spirit lead you and be open to His direction.

Tamara blows her nose really loud.

TAMARA

I'm sorry. I just got caught up.

Joy gives her a hug and some tissue. They continue talking.

TAMARA

Funny you mention Ms. Studimier because on my way over here, I ran into her. I told her about rededicating my life to Christ. I apologized for the embarrassment that I caused her. She said that she forgave me and had been praying for me since I left home. I told her about what happened at the audition and she practically said the same things you're saying. I'm sorry for snapping at you earlier.

JOY

That's okay. Just give yourself some time to readjust…It can be frustrating but it's very rewarding.

TAMARA

Ms. Studimier told me that County College is looking for a ballet instructor and she would be willing to recommend me. It would mean moving back to Newark and starting from scratch. Thank God I at least put some money in the bank for rainy days.

JOY

Brighter days are already here. You got your friends, your family, and a new job – Look at God.

TAMARA

I was so upset about not getting the part, I didn't think about why...Whew I almost missed a blessing.

JOY

God is so good...

TAMARA

Yes, He is and as a matter of fact, I'm gonna go down to County College now.

Tamara gathers her things and walks towards the door.

TAMARA
(waves)

I'll call you later.

JOY

Okay.

Joy chuckles to herself and sits back down on the couch.
She smiles and shakes her head when the telephone rings.

JOY

Hello

MICHAEL'S VOICE

Hey Joy, Whatcha doing?

JOY

Hey Michael. Uhm. Nothing. Tamara just left. What's up?

MICHAEL'S VOICE

Thought you might want to catch a movie.

JOY

Are you asking me out?

MICHAEL'S VOICE

Yeah. Is that a problem?

JOY

Oh no.

MICHAEL'S VOICE

Good. Then I'll pick you up at 7. The movie starts at 9 so we can grab a bite to eat beforehand.

JOY

Okay. I'll see you then.

Joy hangs up the phone. She is excited, she runs to her bedroom to prepare herself. Lights out

SCENE FIVE
HE RESTORES MY SOUL

Lights reveal Rachel dressed in sexy, elegant lingerie. She is putting the finishing touches on a beautiful candle lit table. A Love ballad playing softly in the background. Rafiq enters huffing and puffing. He makes his way through the door placing his briefcase on the floor and his coat on the rack. He walks slowly toward the table. Rachel tries to be calm yet is somewhat nervous as She's not sure what type of reaction Rafiq will have.

RAFIQ

Well, nice of you to come home. Did you enjoy your little weekend getaway?

Rafiq sits at the table and notices its beauty but does not show this. Rachel stops and looks at Rafiq.

RACHEL

I needed some time to think

RAFIQ

Think about what. You sit in this house all day, every day. Why couldn't you THINK here.

RACHEL

Rafiq, I don't want to fight tonight okay. I just want to talk.

RAFIQ

Just fix my plate.

Rachel begins fixing his plate. She places his plate in front of him.

RAFIQ

What, I got to eat by myself now.

Rachel sighs and tries not to become discouraged. She fixes her plate. Rafiq waits until she is done. Rachel extends both her hands inviting Rafiq to hold hands with her.

RACHEL

Can we bless the food?

Rafiq gives her his hands and they bow their heads.

RACHEL

God we thank you for this meal that has been prepared and this time of sharing. Bless it in Jesus Name. Amen

RAFIQ

Amen

They begin eating.

RACHEL

Rafiq, we need to talk.

RAFIQ

So talk

RACHEL
(unsure)

Umm.

RAFIQ

Why don't you just come out and say what you have to say?

RACHEL

These past couple of months have been very stressful on all of us -

RAFIQ

What do you know about stress? You don't do anything around here. This is the first decent meal you've cooked since I don't know when.

RACHEL

That's because you've spent day in and out at the office

RAFIQ

Oh, so keeping a roof over your pretty little head is a problem now, Huh?

RACHEL

Rafiq, I don't want to argue tonight.

RAFIQ

We're *not* arguing, we're merely having a discussion.

RACHEL
(fed up)

Well, guess what. I've had it with you and this discussion.

Rachel gets up from the table and begins walking away.

RAFIQ

Don't you walk away from me woman. What's gotten into you..

Rachel is standing in the living room angry.

RACHEL

I've had it with you.. You hear me. I've had it. You can have your house, your car, your money. None of it matters anymore.

RAFIQ

What are you babbling about?

RACHEL

Look at what you've done to me…Look

Rafiq holds his head down in shame. Rachel begins to cry.

RACHEL

Look at me Rafiq. Look at me.

Rafiq look at her at a loss of words. For the first time he takes notice of the bruises and the tired demeanor of his wife. Rafiq's demeanor seems changed as she speaks.

RACHEL

I'm tired Rafiq. Tired of arguing. Tired of fighting. Tired of retiring to an empty bed night after night. Tired of explaining to our child why daddy isn't home when I know you're sitting up in some bar drinking our lives away. I can't live like this anymore. I can't subject my daughter to this anymore. She's been through and seen too much already (pause) God knows I love you, but I won't stay unless things change.

Rafiq looks at her in disbelief

RAFIQ

You're leaving me?

RACHEL

What other choices do I have?

Rafiq slowly moves toward the couch and sits down. Rachel remains standing in the same position.

RAFIQ

Stay…

RACHEL

What guarantees do I have

RAFIQ

Oh baby...I -- I've lost control. The company started downsizing and cutting back on bonuses. The stocks were down and in order to keep my job I had to the job of the 3 people they fired at no extra pay. The fellas and I would go to happy hour but long after happy hour was over I was still there. Afraid to come home and tell you that you may have to work again. And instead of dealing with my fears, I took them out on you and Precious.

Rafiq sits quietly. He holds his head in his hands and begins to cry. Rachel appears hesitant about going to comfort Rafiq but She goes to his side. However, He is distraught and doesn't notice her.

RAFIQ cont.

Oh God, what have I become?

Rafiq looks up at Rachel

RAFIQ

I can't blame you for wanting to leave me.

RACHEL

I thought about leaving you but I love you.

RAFIQ

You deserve so much better. I've let you down so many times but you always stood by my side. Please don't leave me.

Rafiq realizes what he could have lost. He falls to his knees and while holding on to her legs, begs for forgiveness.

RAFIQ

I'm sorry Rachel...Rachel, baby, I'm sorry. Please... Please..Oh God forgive me.

Rafiq is now crying uncontrollably. Rachel kneels beside him and consoles Rafiq.

RACHEL

I forgive you.

Rachel picks his head up and looks him in the eye

RACHEL

Things will definitely have to change.

RAFIQ

I'll do anything, baby. Anything you want…

Rafiq calms himself. They return to their seats on the couch.

RACHEL

Rafiq, listen, it's not about what I want. It's about what you need. When we met in college both us were wild and having a good time. I was a sorority girl in love with a football player. We drank together, we partied, we had great sex. But when I made the decision to give my life to Christ and you didn't, I had some reservations, but I married you anyway, thinking you would change. Since you didn't change, I had to. I couldn't be the same person anymore…You understand what I mean?

Rafiq nods his head.

RACHEL

…Baby if this thing is going to work, we've got to be on one accord. That means, that if you want to go forward with me, you must accept Jesus Christ as you Lord and Savior. We must take time daily to pray as a couple and family. We are going to counseling to help us deal with stress and learn how to better communicate with one another. Christ must be the center of this marriage or it won't work.

Rafiq looks surprised at the list of demands. Rachel meets his gaze.

RACHEL

You said you want to change, now prove it.

Rachel leaves the living room and goes into the bedroom and closes the door. She gets on her knees. Rafiq seems confused about what to do. He hesitates for a moment. Then He gets on his knees and prays.

RAFIQ

God, if you're as powerful as people say you are, Help me put my life back together. I'm sorry for all the hurt and pain I caused my wife, my daughter, myself.

Rafiq begins to weep. Rachel interceding from the other room.

RAFIQ

I don't want to be like this anymore. I want you to be in control cause obviously I can't handle it myself. So I need you show me what to do. Help me be a better man, husband and father. I need my family but mostly I need you right now. Amen.

Rafiq remains on his knees. Lights out.

SCENE SIX
LOVE DIVINE

Lights reveal Patrick and Amber fully clothed on the bed. She turns to Patrick and looks somewhat in need of his attention.

AMBER

...It's all my fault.

PATRICK

Help me out, start from the beginning.

Amber nudges Patrick and smiles

AMBER

I've been thinking a lot lately

PATRICK

Uh Hmm

AMBER

I realized, with the help of my friends, that in my pursuit of having a child, I've neglected you. Patrick, I'm sorry.

PATRICK

How could I not forgive someone as fine as you are?

Amber blushes.

AMBER

You've been so supportive of me..even in my moments of madness. You're always encouraging me and paying me compliments....I'm blessed to have you in my life.

PATRICK

I just wanted you to understand that you don't have to bear any burden alone. I am always here for you. Whatever I can do to make you happy, I'll do.

Patrick looks into Amber's eyes. He begins to affirm her.

PATRICK

I love you. There's nobody I'd rather spend my life with then you. You are my lover, my friend, my confidant. God created you and you are a beautiful queen and it is my pleasure to serve you. I've missed being with you...

Amber cries.

AMBER

Thank you for loving me so much. I love you and if I don't ever tell you again, I want you to know that I am committed to the growth and happiness of this marriage, *(looking into his eyes)* with or without children.

PATRICK
(smiling)

I hope that doesn't mean we're going to stop trying…. Cause God knows I love trying with you

AMBER

You are so bad.

They share a laugh. Patrick kisses Amber on the forehead. Lights out.

ACT THREE

SCENE ONE
A FAMILY AFFAIR

Lights reveal each married couple, and everyone else seated at the dining room table to have dinner. Amber is pregnant. Everyone is in after five attire and is laughing and talking amongst one another.

Joy stands taps her glass to which they all look and pay attention.

JOY

Well, here we are a year later and so much has changed in each of our lives. As I look around the table, I'm reminded of the healing, deliverance, and restoration that has taken place. The struggles we once had no longer exist. Although our days of struggling are not over, I'm glad we'll never face them alone. It's really great to see all of you. The enemy could have taken us out but I thank God for the grace and mercy He's shown us. And, I thank you for joining in this celebration that marks our commitment to one another and to God. I know that each of us have something to be thankful for, so before we eat, let's just share our heart.

Joy sits and Rachel stands.

RACHEL

First, I would like to thank God, who is the head of this marriage, for His faithfulness. My husband is saved and we are now attending church together. We also attend marriage counseling, where we are learning to be better communicators, lovers and friends. Don't get me wrong -- *(looks at Rafiq)*

We have our moments, but we are doing a lot better. And my baby, Precious is doing well in school and takes after her mommy in dance.

Amber stands.

AMBER

You know this time last year, we as sisters in Christ and friends, made a demand on God. And from that experience, I have learned to trust in Him and fulfill His will for my life. So often the focus is on ourselves and our situations and we forget that God's word instructs us not to worry...having learned some lessons the hard way. I am Godly proud to inform you, that Patrick and I are pregnant.

Amber lifts her glass.

Hallelujah...Hallelujah...Hallelujah

Everyone cheers. They give Amber and Patrick hugs and kisses. Tamara stands

TAMARA

I thank God for changing me. Although there are times when I am tempted to turn back, I have kept my commitment to the Lord. I am a full time instructor of dance at County College and Ms. Studimier has taken me in until I can get enough money to move back into my own place. *(looking into his eyes)*

And it was because of you and your prayers that I reconnected not only with God, but with my family, and each of you. I am learning to receive God's love and respect the temple that He has given me. I'm proud to say that I have remained celibate and with God's help will maintain until I'm married. Thank you Jesus.

Joy stands again.

JOY

I am grateful for the things that God has done for me and the people that He has placed in my path. I don't always understand what He's doing but I know that whatever He does, He does so with my best interest at heart. There have been times when I have become so angry with Him because I didn't get what I wanted. But sometimes, the very thing I wanted, I might not have been ready for. He has taught me how to be intimate with Him and as I grow and develop in the things of God, He continues to bless me...

The doorbell rings. Joy opens the door only to see a large bouquet of beautiful red, pink and white roses in an elegant crystal vase. Joy places her hand over her mouth as she reaches for the roses Michael steps into the doorway, and drops to one knee. Tamara walks over to Joy smiling. Joy, backing up does not notice Tamara as she nearly drops the vase in trying to keep her composure. Tamara takes them away from her and steps out of the way.

MICHAEL

Joy, since the first time we danced, I've wanted to take the rest of my steps with you. You are the epitome of beauty and grace. I respect you....I'm in love with you...and I vow, from this moment on, to cover you in prayer, protect you from any harm, and provide you with your heart's desire.

Michael takes Joy's hand. She kneels in front of Michael and stares into his eyes.

MICHAEL

Joy , I'd like to dance the rest of my life to the music of your love.

Michael pulls the ring from his pocket and presents it to Joy. Joy is ecstatic and overwhelmed.

MICHAEL

Will you take this God-fearing, humble, and imperfect man, to be your husband?

JOY
(through tears)

Yes....yes

Joy and Michael embrace and He places the ring on her finger. She cries in Michael's arms. Everyone else begins to cheer. Michael escorts Joy to the middle of the floor. A Romantic Ballad and They dance. Rafiq and Rachel, Patrick and Amber join them while Tamara prepares the meal After the dance, All Couples return to the table and are seated. Tamara stands.

TAMARA

Well in honor or Joy and Michael's engagement, let's raise our glasses together. To second, third, and fourth chances....

AMBER

To trusting God every step of the way

PATRICK

To making our dreams a reality

RACHEL

To love, faith, and perseverance

RAFIQ

To mended hearts, minds, and spirits

MICHAEL

To…

PRECIOUS

Hey what about me?

MICHAEL

I'm sorry Precious

PRECIOUS

That's okay

Precious raises her cup

PRECIOUS

To a big God who hears little prayers

MICHAEL

To new beginnings

JOY

To God's perfect timing

Everyone toasts and then hugs and takes their seat.

AMBER

Would someone like to bless the food?!

RAFIQ

Good food. Good Meat. Bless God. Let's eat.

PATRICK, MICHAEL

Amen.

The women shake their heads in shame as they share a laugh and begin eating.

JOY

Oh, by the way, as a special treat, Tamara has choreographed a dance that we would like to present to you as an expression of our appreciation and a sign of our victory.

Amber, Rachel, Precious, Joy, Tamara all rise from the table. Lights out.

SCENE TWO
THE DANCER'S PRAYER

The women take their position on the stage and follow Tamara as she leads them in a dance to the hymn What A Friend We Have In Jesus. When complete, they all gather in a circle and are positioned as statuesque sculpture or work of art center stage. Blackout. End of play.

ACKNOWLEDGEMENTS

First and foremost, I thank God for hearing and answering prayer...

To Catina Mumford who encouraged me to share this piece with the drama ministry...

To Bishop George and Lady Mary Searight of Abundant Life Family Worship Church (New Brunswick, NJ) for allowing us the opportunity to have an unforgettable praise and worship experience that can be expressed through the Vision Drama Ministry...

To Carol and Ashley Hall, Thera Ward, Yetunde Hart and the cast and crew who brought the piece alive in its premier on the George Street Playhouse stage...

To my mother, Geneva Morrison, and my sister, April Morrison for always being there to support me...

You are forever engraved upon my heart for making this a dream come true...

Grace and peace be unto you, from God our Father and the Lord Jesus Christ!!!